Scared Little Red Riding Hood

SUE NICHOLSON

Illustrated by LAURA BRENLLA

Once Upon A Time...

...there was a misty blue mountain.

Quarto is the authority on a wide range of topics.

Quarto educates, entertains and enriches the lives of our readers—enthusiasts and lovers of hands-on living.

www.quartoknows.com

Author: Sue Nicholson
Illustrator: Laura Brenlla
Designer: Victoria Kimonidou
Editor: Emily Pither

© 2019 Quarto Publishing plc

Sue Nicholson has asserted her right to be identified as the author of this work.
Illustrations © Laura Brenlla c/o Good Illustration Ltd 2019

First Published in 2019 by QED Publishing, an imprint of The Quarto Group.
The Old Brewery, 6 Blundell Street, London N7 9BH, United Kingdom.
T (0)20 7700 6700 F (0)20 7700 8066
www.QuartoKnows.com

A catalogue record for this book is available from the British Library.

ISBN 978-0-7112-4472-6

Manufactured in Shenzhen, China PP072019

9 8 7 6 5 4 3 2 1

Below the misty blue mountain
was a wild, dark forest and by the
wild, dark forest was a village.

The village had a stream and a duck pond and an old red apple tree and
it was home to **Little Red Riding Hood** and her fairytale friends.

Little Red Riding Hood lived with her grandmother in a tiny cottage at the edge of the **wild, dark forest.**

Yikes!

Little Red Riding Hood was scared of almost everything.

She was scared of spiders.

Uh-oh!

She was scared of the dark.

woof!

Eek!

She was scared of loud noises that made her jump.

But most of all, she was scared of the wild, dark forest, with its sudden **creaks** and **groans.** She didn't like the way the wind **snapped** at the twigs and **rustled** through the leaves.

"Scared Little Red Riding Hood!" teased
Jack and Goldilocks when she wouldn't
play with them at the forest's edge.

One night, Little Red Riding Hood heard a **wolf** howling.

A-woooOOOO

A-woooOOOO

"Did you hear a wolf?" she asked Jack and Goldilocks the next day.

"Don't be silly," they laughed. "There aren't any wolves in the forest."

"It sounded big," said Little Red Riding Hood.

"With **great big eyes** to see you," teased Jack. "And **great big ears** to hear you," teased Goldilocks.

"And **great big teeth** to gobble me up," trembled Little Red Riding Hood as she walked home from school.

"Did you hear a wolf howling last night?" Little Red Riding Hood asked Griselda, who was gardening.

"My grandmother can't hear very well and my friends say there aren't any wolves in the forest."

"Well, there are wolves in the forest and, yes, *I* did hear it,"
said Griselda, "but don't be scared. Wolves usually stay
far away from people. It won't come near the village."

"*I* thought the wolf sounded sad," added Griselda.

As Little Red Riding Hood lay in bed that night listening
to the wolf's howl, she realised Griselda was right.

The wolf did sound sad and she wondered why.

The following day, Little Red Riding Hood heard a **rustle** and a **yelp** in the leaves by the wood pile. She took a step closer and
OUT POPPED A WOLF!

But it wasn't a scary wolf with great big eyes and great big ears and great big teeth.

It was a little lost wolf cub.

"That's your mother howling for you, isn't it?"
whispered Little Red Riding Hood.
"Do you need me to take you back to her?"

The tiny cub licked her hand.

Even though she didn't feel very brave, Little Red Riding Hood put the tiny wolf cub in her basket. Then she set off through the trees, following the mother wolf's howls...

A-wOOOOOOO

A-wOOOOOOO

The forest was just as dark and wild as she'd imagined.

"Don't be scared, little wolf," whispered Little Red Riding Hood, as the leaves **rustled** and the branches **creaked** and **groaned**.

On and on went Little Red Riding Hood until,
at last, she came to a clearing...

Gulp!

... and there was
the
BIG
WOLF!

She had great big eyes and great big ears
and great big teeth – big enough to gobble
me up, gulped Little Red Riding Hood.

A-WOOOOOOOO

cried the wolf as her cub jumped out
of Little Red Riding Hood's basket.

A-WOOOOOOO

cried the cub as he scampered
towards his mother.

Little Red Riding Hood smiled as the wolf nuzzled her little cub's face and licked his fur.

The wolf gazed at Little Red Riding Hood and lowered her head, as if to say 'thank you'. Then she and her cub padded away through the trees.

Little Red Riding Hood ran home. She was glad she'd been brave enough to reunite the lost cub with his mother.

She realised she wasn't quite so scared of the wild, dark forest anymore. Not now she'd faced a wolf.

Jack and Goldilocks stopped teasing her, too,
when she told them what she'd done.
"Wow! You're **Brave** Little Red Riding Hood!"
they cried.

(She was still scared
of spiders, though!)

Next Steps

Discussion points

Discuss with the children what the word 'bravery' means and what an amazing character Scared Little Red Riding Hood is for overcoming her fears and showing such bravery when the little wolf cub needed help. Discuss with the children which fears are real, like the wolf, and which might be imaginary. Tell the children what you are most scared of and give them an example of when you overcame your fears and were brave! Remember to reinforce that it is ok to be scared, but sometimes being brave means that you can do things that you might otherwise not do. Below are suggestions for discussion points about the story. These will help the children with their comprehension skills, as well as developing their understanding of fear and bravery.

- Can you describe what it is about the forest that makes Red Riding Hood scared? What words does the author use to make the forest sound scary?
  - Was Red Riding Hood's fear real or imaginary?
- Why do you think that the wolf was sad?
  - Why do you think it's important to help others when they feel sad?
- What does the word 'courage' mean? How was Red Riding Hood brave?
  - Can you think of any ways you could try to overcome your fears?
- How was Griselda helpful?
  - Can you think of a time that someone helped you when you were scared?
- Think about the ending of the story. How was it happy for everyone?

Forest painting

Give each child a sheet of plain sugar paper, a paintbrush, a straw and brown, green, blue, red and black paint. Ask them to paint a background using brown and green paint for the forest floor and blue paint for the sky. Once this has dried, the children can blow paint trees with their straw and the black paint to make the forest look scary and dense like the illustrations in the book. Leave the paintings to dry flat - don't pick them up as the paint will run. Then encourage the children to use red and green paint to splatter paint some flowers, toadstools and leaves on the floor of the forest. Once the painting is dry, give each child a small colour photocopied picture of Scared Little Red Riding Hood and the wolf cub. Ask them to stick them to their painting.